My Holiday in

Italy

Susie Brooks

WAYLAND

First published in 2008 by Wayland

Copyright © Wayland 2008

Wayland
338 Euston Road
London NW1 3BH

Wayland Australia
Level 17/207 Kent Street
Sydney NSW 2000

Senior Editor: Claire Shanahan
Designer: Elaine Wilkinson
Map artwork: David le Jars

Brooks, Susie
My holiday in Italy
1. Vacations - Italy - Juvenile literature 2. Recreation - Italy -
Juvenile literature 3. Italy - Juvenile literature 4. Italy - Social life
and customs - 21st century - Juvenile literature I. Title II. Italy
914.5'0493

ISBN 978 0 7502 5328 4

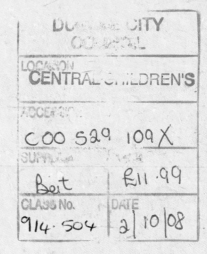

Cover: The Leaning Tower of Pisa © Reuters/Corbis; Italian footballer Fabio Cannavaro (left) in a Euro 2008
qualifier against Georgia © Zurab Kutsikidze/epa/Corbis.

p6: © Walter Bibikow/JAI/Corbis; p7: © Wayland Picture Library; p8, title page: © Peter Adams/Getty; p9: ©
Heather Perry/National Geographic/Getty; p10: © travelstock44/Alamy; p11: © Wayland Picture Library; p12: ©
Travelpix Ltd; p13: © Richard Ross/Getty; p14: © Sergio Pitamitz/zefa/Corbis; p15: © UKraft/Alamy; p16: ©
Reuters/Corbis; p17: © Philip & Karen Smith/Lonely Planet Images/Getty; p18: © Vittoriano Rastelli/Corbis; p19:
© De Agostini/Getty; p20: © Dennis Flaherty/Getty; p22: © Robert Harding Picture Library Ltd/Alamy; p23: ©
Wayland Picture Library; p24: © Chuck Pefley/Alamy; p25: © Pool/Immaginazione/Corbis; p26: © Zurab
Kutsikidze/epa/Corbis; p27: © Schlegelmilch/Corbis; ©; p28: © John Slater/Corbis; p29: © Marco
Bucco/Reuters/Corbis; Rita Storey/Wishlist; p31: © Wayland Picture Library.

Printed in China

Wayland is a division of Hachette Children's Books, an Hachette Livre UK company.

www.hachettelivre.co.uk

Contents

This is Italy!

It's easy to spot Italy on a map because it is shaped like a boot! Italy is a country in southern Europe. Most people travel here by aeroplane.

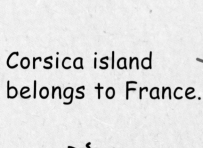

Corsica island belongs to France.

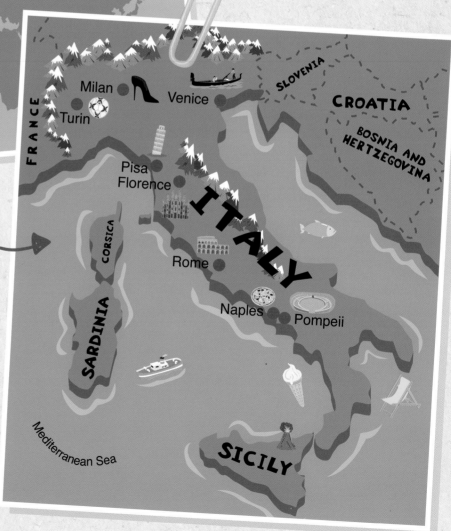

This is the Piazza Navona, a square in Italy's capital city, Rome.

The north and south of Italy are very different. But you'll notice things that are typically Italian, like the type of food and the language people speak.

It was fun grabbing our suitcases from the conveyor belt at the airport.

Speak Italian!

good morning
buon giorno (bon-ji-**or**-no)

good afternoon
buona sera (bwon-a-**sair**-a)

goodbye
arrivederci (a-ree-vi-**dair**-chee)

Fun for all seasons

A lot of people travel to Italy for its summer sunshine. The weather can be very hot, especially in the south.

The island of Sicily is popular for beach holidays, even in winter.

In September, we got soaked by a massive thunderstorm!

Weather in Rome

July – take suncream
October – take an umbrella!

Italy's mountains
are cooler and
wetter. People
come skiing here
in the winter snow.
Spring and autumn
are good times
for sightseeing.

Cycling holidays
are fun in spring,
but beware of
the hills!

Be at home

This is the town of Positano on the Amalfi coast, south-west Italy.

Italy has many **resort** towns, built especially for **tourists** to stay in. There are also hotels in all the cities.

We stayed in a bed and breakfast – it was like being in someone's house!

8

You can make as much noise as you like in your own villa pool! This one is in the hilly region of **Tuscany**.

Some families rent holiday houses, called **villas**, in the countryside. If you're adventurous, you might prefer to camp.

Speak Italian!

bedroom
stanza (**stan**-za)

bathroom
bagno (**ban**-yo)

toilet
gabinetto (ga-bin-**ett**-o)

9

Twisty travel

Cars, buses and scooters make lots of traffic in Rome.

Driving around Italy is a good way to see the country – but the mountain roads can be very wiggly! There are tunnels through the Alps to other parts of Europe.

Speak Italian!

train
treno (**tre**-no)
bus
autobus (**out**-o-boos)
ticket
biglietto (bee-lee-**ett**-o)

Fast trains and motorways
take people from city to city.
Some tourists hire scooters or
motorbikes to travel around.

In the watery
city of Venice,
there are no
cars but lots
of boats.

We went on a **gondola** in
Venice. The man paddling
sang us songs.

Roaming in Rome

A visit to Rome is like travelling through time. The city was built by the Romans more than 2,000 years ago, but it has changed a lot since then.

People say if you drop a coin in the Trevi Fountain you'll return to Rome one day!

Things to see...

The **Colosseum** – where Romans fought with wild animals

Ciao da Roma!

Roma – Castel Sant'Angelo

The Capuchin crypt – full of skulls and bones

Castel Sant Angelo – climb the spiral ramp to the top

Be a Roman!

Take a day trip to Ostia Antica and...

- walk along a Roman street
- see ancient baths and toilets
- visit a Roman snack bar

City trips

You might stay in one of Italy's other great cities.

Spot the houses on the Ponte Vecchio (Old Bridge).

Florence

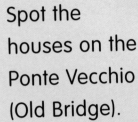

Famous for: art and buildings
You can:
- climb the Campanile bell tower or the huge Duomo dome.
- pose next to **Michelangelo's** famous statue David.
- shop for gold on the Ponte Vecchio.

Venice

Famous for: canals and Carnivale
You can:
- explore secret streets by boat.
- feed pigeons in St Mark's Square.
- watch glassblowers on Murano island.

Milan

Famous for: fashion and football
You can:
- see amazing inventions by **Leonardo da Vinci**.
- Take a day trip to Gardaland – Italy's favourite fun park.

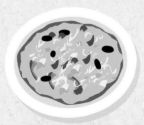

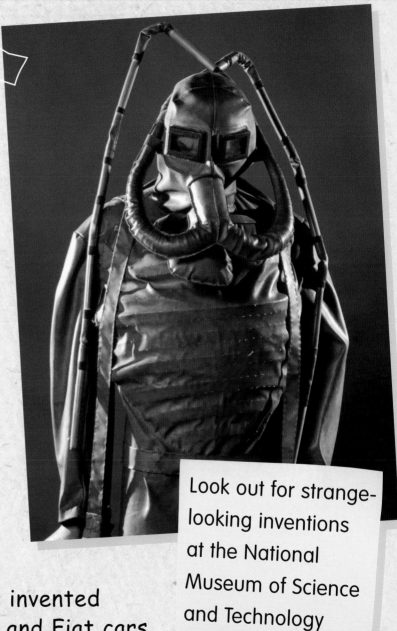

Look out for strange-looking inventions at the National Museum of Science and Technology in Milan!

Naples – where pizza was invented
Turin – for winter sports and Fiat cars
Bologna – home of spaghetti bolognese

Special sights

These are some other places people like to visit in Italy.

North

• The Leaning Tower of Pisa – it hasn't fallen over yet!
• Cinque Terre ('five lands') – five cliff-top villages you can visit by boat

Fun sculpture parks

• The 'monster garden' at Bomarzo near Rome
• Pinocchio Park in Collodi, Tuscany

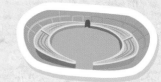

• Pompeii – a town buried when a volcano, Mount Vesuvius, **erupted** nearly 2,000 years ago. Now you can run around the ancient ruins!

• Matera – a mysterious place where people still live in prehistoric caves
• Capri – a magical island with a bright blue grotto

Holiday tip

You can see all of Italy's most famous sights in one mini-land at Italia in Miniatura near Rimini.

17

Wild Italy

People love to explore Italy's countryside. In the Alps, there are beautiful lakes and forests where wolves and bears hide.

You might spot a porcupine in the forests near Pisa.

I went up in a cable car in the mountains – it was scary looking down!

You can watch the Stromboli volcano erupting – from a safe distance!

Further south, you'll see farmland and hills with villages perched at the top. Near Italy's 'toe' there are islands with volcanoes.

Crops to spot

- Olives, for making oil
- Grapes, for making wine
- Wheat, for making pasta
- Oranges, lemons and tomatoes

Buon apetito!

You have probably eaten Italian food – but it tastes better in Italy! Pizza, pasta and ice cream were all invented here. Try as many different sorts as you can.

People say Italian ice cream (gelato) is the best in the world. It can be hard to choose the flavour you want!

Italian pasta is often topped with local cheeses such as mozzarella and parmesan. Bread comes with each meal, so you can mop your plate clean!

Every pasta shape has its own name.

Vermicelli
'little worms'

Conchiglie
'shells'

Spaghetti
'little string'

Linguine
'little tongues'

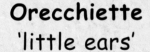

Orecchiette
'little ears'

Farfalle
'butterflies'

On the menu

risotto (ri-**zot**-to) -
a creamy rice dish

gnocchi (n-**yock**-ee) -
little dumplings
served in sauce

tiramisu (ti-ra-mee-**soo**) -
a creamy coffee and
chocolate dessert

Get shopping!

You need to change your money to euros in Italy. Then you can buy **souvenirs** to take home. Look for things that remind you of your holiday.

Craft stalls like these are good for buying presents.

Italians do most of their everyday shopping in small shops and markets. People on holiday in Italy buy a lot of leather and designer clothes.

The Galleria in Milan has lots of shops and cafés.

Speak Italian!

please
per favore (pair-fa-**vor**-ay)

thank you
grazie (**grat**-zee-ay)

how much is it?
cuanto cuesta?
(cw-**an**-toh cw-**es**-ta?)

23

Italian life

There's a saying that goes, 'When in Rome, do as the Romans do'. If you do as the Italians do, you will probably stay up late and have fun with your family.

You might go to a restaurant for a treat in the evening!

Special post

Send a postcard from Vatican City! The **Pope** lives here – it is a separate country in Rome, with its own special stamps and post office.

Most Italians are **Roman Catholics**. Sundays are rest days when many shops close and some people go to church.

Crowds gather in the grounds of Vatican City to be blessed by the Pope.

At play

Going to a football match is an exciting way to join in Italian life. Italians are football mad! Most people support their local team.

Look out for the Italian team colours – they play in bright blue!

Other popular sports include basketball, cycling and motor racing. People from all over the world come skiing and snowboarding in the Alps mountains in winter.

Italy is home of the Ferrari racing car.

I tried windsurfing at Lake Garda – I kept wobbling over and falling in!

Costume crazy!

If you like dressing up, go to Italy during Carnivale! This exciting festival marks the beginning of the Christian time of **Lent**.

People wear amazing masks at the Carnivale festival in Venice!

Different regions of Italy hold their own festivals at different times of year. A famous one is Il Palio, which happens in Siena in July and September.

Il Palio is a bareback horse race around the city square.

Famous fiestas

~~Easter Day~~ for fantastic ~~fireworks in~~ Florence	~~Easter Monday~~ for cheese-rolling ~~races in Panecale~~	~~Epiphany~~ (6 January) for presents from La Befana (the Italian female Santa!)	

Make it yourself

Make this Leaning Tower of Pizza to share with your friends!

You will need:

You will need:

- long stick of bread
- chopped tomatoes (tinned)
- grated mozzarella cheese
- toppings – e.g. ham, sweetcorn, mushrooms, peppers, cheese – you choose!
- Italian herbs
- olive oil.

The Leaning Tower of Pizza

1. Ask an adult to cut the bread into slices about 1cm thick.

2. Spread each slice with chopped tomatoes and cover with grated cheese.

3. Now add different toppings to each piece of bread – arrange them in patterns if you like! Then sprinkle with Italian herbs and drizzle with olive oil.

4. Ask an adult to bake your mini-pizzas until they are crispy.

5. When the pizzas are out of the oven, let them cool for a minute. Then pile them up on a plate – and there's your Leaning Tower of Pizza!

Cheese + tomato = Margherita

Spinach + egg = Fiorentina

4 types of cheese = Quattro formaggi

TIP: Place the smallest piece of bread on top so it doesn't topple your tower.

Useful words

Colosseum The ancient theatre in Rome.

erupt When a volcano throws out hot rock or ash.

gondola A long, narrow boat found on the canals of Venice.

Lent The 40 days leading up to Easter when Christians traditionally give something up.

Leonardo da Vinci A great Italian artist and inventor who lived from 1452–1519. His famous paintings include the Last Supper in Milan.

Michelangelo A famous Italian artist who lived from 1475–1564. He painted the Sistine Chapel ceiling in Rome – it took him four years!

Pope The leader of the Roman Catholic church.

resort A place for holidaymakers, with hotels and other facilities.

Roman Catholic A type of Christian.

souvenir Something you take home to remind you of somewhere you have been.

tourist Someone who is on holiday or sightseeing.

Tuscany A beautiful, hilly region in western Italy.

villa A home in the countryside.